Fun Food for Cool Cooks

Oodle Doodles Tuna Noodle

AND OTHER SALAD RECIPES

by Kristi Johnson

Capstone press

Mankato, Minnesota

Snap Books are published by Capstone Press,
151 Good Counsel Drive, P.O. Box 669, Mankato, Minnesota 56002.
www.capstonepress.com

Library of Congress Cataloging-in-Publication Data
Johnson, Kristi.
  Oodle doodles tuna noodle and other salad recipes / by Kristi Johnson.
  p. cm. — (Snap books. Fun food for cool cooks)
  Summary: "Provides fun and unique recipes for salads, including potato salad, fruit salad, and
tuna salad. Includes easy instructions and a helpful tools glossary with photos" — Provided by publisher.
  Includes bibliographical references and index.
  ISBN-13: 978-1-4296-1341-5 (hardcover)
  ISBN-10: 1-4296-1341-6 (hardcover)
  1. Salads — Juvenile literature. I. Title. II. Series.

TX740.J62 2008
641.8'3 — dc22   2007031484

Editor: Kathryn Clay
Designer: Juliette Peters
Photo Stylists: Kelly Garvin and Sarah Schuette

Photo Credits:
All principle photography in this book by Capstone Press/Karon Dubke
Capstone Press/TJ Thoraldson Digital Photography, cooking utensils (all)
Tami Johnson, 32

1 2 3 4 5 6 13 12 11 10 09 08

TABLE OF CONTENTS

PAGE 10

PAGE 14

PAGE 18

PAGE 22

PAGE 24

PAGE 26

INTRODUCTION

SEEING STARS

When choosing a recipe, let the stars be your guide! Just follow this chart to find recipes that fit your cooking comfort level.

EASY: ★ ☆ ☆
MEDIUM: ★ ★ ☆
ADVANCED: ★ ★ ★

When the menu says "salad," what image comes to mind? Health food? Boring iceberg lettuce? Fat free dressing? Well forget all of that. Salads can be fun and delicious. In fact, salads can be on the menu for lunch, dinner, and dessert! There are pizza salads, noodle salads, and even salads with candy! There is no limit to what you can do with a salad. If you're looking for a meal, a side dish, or just a snack, there is a salad for you. With fun recipes like these, when you hear "salad," you'll say "Mmmmm!"

METRIC CONVERSION GUIDE

United States	Metric
¼ teaspoon	1.2 mL
½ teaspoon	2.5 mL
1 teaspoon	5 mL
1 tablespoon	15 mL
¼ cup	60 mL
⅓ cup	80 mL
½ cup	120 mL
⅔ cup	160 mL
¾ cup	175 mL
1 cup	240 mL
1 quart	1 liter
1 ounce	30 grams
2 ounces	55 grams
4 ounces	110 grams
½ pound	225 grams
1 pound	455 grams

Fahrenheit	Celsius
325°	160°
350°	180°
375°	190°
400°	200°
425°	220°
450°	230°

All good cooks know that a successful recipe takes a little preparation. Use this handy checklist to save time when working in the kitchen.

BEFORE YOU BEGIN

READ YOUR RECIPE

Once you've chosen a recipe, carefully read over it. The recipe will go smoothly if you understand the steps and techniques.

CHECK THE PANTRY

Make sure you have all the ingredients on hand. After all, it's hard to bake cookies without sugar!

DRESS FOR SUCCESS

Wear an apron to keep your clothes clean. Roll up long sleeves. Tie long hair back so it doesn't get in your way — or in the food.

GET OUT YOUR TOOLS

Sort through the cupboards and gather all the tools you'll need to prepare the recipe. Can't tell a spatula from a mixing spoon? No problem. Refer to the handy tools glossary in this book.

PREPARE YOUR INGREDIENTS

A little prep time at the start will pay off in the end.

- Rinse any fresh ingredients such as fruit and vegetables.
- Use a peeler to remove the peel from foods like apples and carrots.
- Cut up fresh ingredients as called for in the recipe. Keep an adult nearby when using a knife to cut or chop food.
- Measure all the ingredients and place them in separate bowls or containers so they're ready to use. Remember to use the correct measuring cups for dry and wet ingredients.

PREHEAT THE OVEN

If you're baking treats, it's important to preheat the oven. Cakes, cookies, and breads bake better in an oven that's heated to the correct temperature.

The kitchen may be unfamiliar turf for many young chefs. Here's a list of trusty tips to help keep you safe in the kitchen.

KITCHEN SAFETY

ADULT HELPERS

Ask an adult to help. Whether you're chopping, mixing, or baking, you'll want an adult nearby to lend a hand or answer questions.

FIRST AID

Keep a first aid kit handy in the kitchen, just in case you have an accident. A basic first aid kit contains bandages, a cream or spray to treat burns, alcohol wipes, gauze, and a small scissors.

WASH UP

Before starting any recipe, be sure to wash your hands. Wash your hands again after working with messy ingredients like jelly or syrup.

HANDLE HABITS

Turn handles of cooking pots toward the center of the stove. You don't want anyone to bump into a handle that's sticking off the stove.

USING KNIVES

It's always best to get an adult's help when using knives. Choose a knife that's the right size for both your hands and the food. Hold the handle firmly when cutting, and keep your fingers away from the blade.

COVER UP

Always wear oven mitts or use pot holders to take hot trays and pans out of the oven.

KEEP IT CLEAN

Spills and drips are bound to happen. Wipe up messes with a paper towel or clean kitchen towel to keep your workspace tidy.

The next time you're looking for an easy salad to make, go fish! This fun twist on tuna salad will blow your guests out of the water.

OODLE DOODLES TUNA NOODLE SALAD

WHAT YOU NEED

•• Ingredients

½ medium onion
2 celery stalks
1 cup of your favorite noodles
1 (6-ounce) can white chunk tuna, drained
2 teaspoons salt
2 teaspoons pepper
½ cup mayonnaise
1 cup frozen peas, thawed
1 cup chow mein noodles

•• Tools

cutting board

sharp knife

saucepan

colander

large mixing bowl

mixing spoon

1 On a cutting board, chop up onion and celery with a sharp knife.

2 In a saucepan, cook noodles according to package directions.

3 Drain the noodles in a colander and set them aside to cool.

4 In a large mixing bowl, combine tuna, salt, pepper, chopped onion, chopped celery, mayonnaise, and peas with a mixing spoon.

5 Add cooked noodles to the mixing bowl and stir.

6 Just before serving, sprinkle chow mein noodles on top of the salad.

Noodle Knowledge

Why use plain old elbow macaroni when there are so many fun shapes to choose from? Shells work great for tuna noodle salad. So does fiori (flower-shaped pasta), rotelle (wagon wheel-shaped pasta), or farfalle (pasta that is shaped like butterflies). There is even pasta called bumbola that's shaped like bumblebees!

On a hot summer day, cool off with this refreshing and colorful fruit salad. It's quick and easy to make, so you can be back on the beach or in the water in no time.

DIFFICULTY LEVEL: ★ ☆ ☆
SERVING SIZE: 6

RAINBOW FRUIT SALAD

WHAT YOU NEED

●● *Ingredients*

1 small seedless watermelon
1 cantaloupe
1 can pineapple chunks
1 pint strawberries
1 pint blueberries
1 pint raspberries
1 cup pastel mini marshmallows

●● *Tools*

cutting board   sharp knife   melon baller

large mixing bowl   mixing spoon

colander   paring knife

1 On a cutting board, cut the watermelon in half with a sharp knife. Use a melon baller to scoop out the inside of the watermelon. Place the melon balls in a large mixing bowl.

2 On the cutting board, cut the cantaloupe in half. Scoop out the seeds with a mixing spoon and throw seeds away. Use the melon baller to scoop out the inside of the cantaloupe. Add the melon balls to the mixing bowl.

4 Drain pineapple into a colander and add to the mixing bowl.

5 On the cutting board, cut the green tops off of the strawberries with a paring knife. Cut the strawberries in half and place into the mixing bowl.

6 Add blueberries, raspberries, and marshmallows to the mixing bowl. Mix all the ingredients together with the mixing spoon.

Tasty Tip

For more fruit flavor, add bananas to this salad. Bananas quickly turn brown after peeling. If you don't plan to eat this right away, add bananas 10–15 minutes before serving. If you do plan to eat this salad right away, peel and slice bananas and mix in with the rest of the salad.

11

Are you headed to a barbeque or beach picnic?
No summer get-together is complete without a big bowl
of potato salad. Try this sweet variation of a classic dish.

DIFFICULTY LEVEL: ★ ★ ☆
SERVING SIZE: 6–8

SWEET SUMMER POTATO SALAD

WHAT YOU NEED

●● *Ingredients*

4 large potatoes
3 hard-boiled eggs
1 cup green grapes, cut in half
1 teaspoon salt
1 teaspoon pepper
½ cup mayonnaise
¼ cup apple juice
2 teaspoons mustard
½ cup chow mein noodles

●● *Tools*

cutting board   vegetable peeler   paring knife

saucepan   fork   colander

large mixing bowl   rubber scraper

1 On a cutting board, use a vegetable peeler to remove potato skins. Cut potatoes into small pieces with a paring knife.

2 Put the potatoes into a saucepan. Fill the pan with enough water to cover the potatoes. Boil the potatoes until they are tender when you poke them with a fork (about 10 minutes).

3 Drain potatoes in a colander. Be careful. The steam will be very hot. Allow the potatoes to cool.

4 Peel hard-boiled eggs (see sidebar). Slice eggs into small pieces with the paring knife. Put egg pieces into a large mixing bowl.

5 Add cooled potatoes, grapes, salt, pepper, mayonnaise, apple juice, and mustard to the mixing bowl. Fold ingredients together with a rubber scraper.

6 Sprinkle chow mein noodles on top of the salad. Keep the salad cold until ready to serve. Refrigerate leftovers immediately.

Hard-boiled Egg Tips

1 Place eggs in a saucepan. Add enough water to cover the eggs, and cook on high until water starts to boil (about 10 minutes).

2 Reduce to medium heat and cook an additional 5 minutes.

3 Use a slotted spoon to remove the eggs. Place eggs in a bowl of ice water for 10–15 minutes.

4 When the eggs are cool, peel off the shells.

With a combination of whipped topping, juicy apples, and sweet candy bars, this can hardly be called a salad. Fill your plate, because this dish will go fast!

DIFFICULTY LEVEL: ★ ★ ☆
SERVING SIZE: 6–8

CANDY BAR SALAD

WHAT YOU NEED

●● Ingredients

2 chocolate bars
3 large Granny Smith apples
1 (8-ounce) container whipped topping
¼ cup peanuts
¼ cup caramel ice cream topping

●● Tools

large mixing bowl

cutting board

vegetable peeler

paring knife

rubber scraper

1 Break candy bars into small pieces. Put candy pieces in a large mixing bowl.

2 On a cutting board, use a vegetable peeler to remove all the skin on the apples.

3 Slice the apples into fourths with a paring knife. Cut out the core and dice apple into small cubes. Add apple cubes to the mixing bowl.

4 Scoop whipped topping into the bowl with a rubber scraper.

5 Add peanuts and stir ingredients together with the rubber scraper.

6 Drizzle caramel on top of mixture before serving.

Tasty Tips

This recipe is easy to change and make your own. Just substitute chocolate covered peanuts for the chocolate bars and peanuts. If you don't have caramel ice cream topping, use chocolate covered caramel candy. See what fun combinations you can create.

Do you love pizza but find it hard to eat your veggies?
This recipe combines the two for a tasty pizza salad.

PEPPERONI PIZZA SALAD

WHAT YOU NEED

•• *Ingredients*

4 cups romaine or iceberg lettuce
½ cup cherry tomatoes
1 small can sliced black olives
1 small package sliced pepperoni
½ cup shredded mozzarella cheese
½ cup Italian dressing

•• *Tools*

cutting board   sharp knife

large mixing bowl   mixing spoon

1 On a cutting board, chop lettuce into bite-sized pieces with a sharp knife. Put lettuce into a large mixing bowl.

2 On the cutting board, cut tomatoes in half. Add tomatoes to the mixing bowl.

3 Add sliced olives, pepperoni, and mozzarella cheese to the bowl.

4 Pour dressing over salad. Mix ingredients together with a mixing spoon.

Shopping for Toppings

Just like pizza, you can add a variety of different ingredients to this salad. Don't like pepperoni? Just add some chicken and bacon. Try a Hawaiian-style pizza salad with ham and pineapple. For veggie pizza salad, add fresh mushrooms, bell peppers, and green olives. You can even spice up your salad by adding fresh basil and oregano.

This south of the border favorite can be served as a side dish or even as the main course. Spicy and full of flavor, this taco salad will be a fiesta for your taste buds.

mexican fiesta salad

WHAT YOU NEED

●● *Ingredients*

1 pound ground beef
1 packet taco seasoning
½ head iceberg lettuce
2 cups shredded cheddar cheese
1 bag tortilla chips, crushed
½ cup French salad dressing
1 cup cherry tomatoes

●● *Tools*

skillet spatula colander

cutting board sharp knife large mixing bowl

mixing spoon

1 In a skillet, cook ground beef on medium-high for 10–14 minutes or until hamburger browns. Use a spatula to stir meat as it cooks.

2 Using a colander, drain fat from meat. Return meat to the skillet. Add taco seasoning to the meat according to directions on packet. Allow meat to cool.

3 On a cutting board, cut lettuce into small pieces with a sharp knife. Put lettuce into a large mixing bowl.

4 Add shredded cheese, crushed tortilla chips, and French dressing to the mixing bowl.

5 Add meat to the mixing bowl. Mix the ingredients with a mixing spoon.

6 On the cutting board, cut tomatoes in half with the sharp knife. Fold tomatoes into the salad.

Tasty Tip

Feel like spicing it up a bit? Add 2 teaspoons of your favorite hot sauce. This will give your Mexican Fiesta Salad a spicier flavor.

Say "cheese!" This recipe takes a classic meal and turns it into a cheesy salad. Use your favorite cheese crackers or even potato chips to give this salad an extra crunch.

DIFFICULTY LEVEL: ★ ★ ☆
SERVING SIZE: 6

TRIPLE CHEESE AND MACARONI SALAD

WHAT YOU NEED

●● Ingredients

1 box macaroni and cheese dinner mix
½ cup cherry tomatoes
¼ cup mayonnaise
½ cup cheddar cheese crumbles
½ cup cheese crackers

●● Tools

saucepan

colander

cutting board

paring knife

large mixing bowl

rubber scraper

1 In a saucepan, cook macaroni noodles according to package directions.

2 Drain the noodles in a colander and set them aside to cool. Do not add cheese packet, milk, or butter.

3 On a cutting board, cut tomatoes in half with a paring knife.

4 In a large mixing bowl, stir together cheese packet and mayonnaise with a rubber scraper.

5 Add noodles to the mixing bowl and stir.

6 Add cherry tomatoes and cheese crumbles to the bowl. Gently stir all ingredients together.

7 Sprinkle cheese crackers on top of salad before serving.

Presidential Party Food

Former president Thomas Jefferson served macaroni and cheese in the White House in 1802. Some people even believe Thomas Jefferson invented macaroni and cheese.

A salad is all about veggies, right? Not when the salad combines apples, grapes, walnuts, and gummy worms. With so much flavor and fun, this salad tastes more like dessert.

DIFFICULTY LEVEL: ★ ★ ☆
SERVING SIZE: 6

APPLE AND WORM SALAD

WHAT YOU NEED

●● *Ingredients*

3 large apples
    (1 Granny Smith, 1 Fiji, 1 Honey Crisp)
¼ cup raisins
½ cup red seedless grapes, cut in half
½ cup green seedless grapes, cut in half
½ cup chopped walnuts
10 gummy worms
½ cup yogurt (plain or vanilla)
1 tablespoon lemon juice
1 tablespoon sugar

●● *Tools*

cutting board

paring knife

large mixing bowl

small bowl

mixing spoon

1 On a cutting board, slice apples into fourths with a paring knife.

2 Cut out the cores and dice apples into small cubes. Place apple cubes in a large mixing bowl.

3 Add raisins, grapes, walnuts, and gummy worms to the mixing bowl.

4 In a small bowl, stir together yogurt, lemon juice, and sugar with a mixing spoon.

5 Add yogurt mixture to the large mixing bowl. Stir ingredients together with the mixing spoon.

Apple Picking

While this recipe has a combination of sweet, tart, and crisp apples, you can use any mix of apples. Buy a few different kinds of apples and see which ones you like best. Use your favorites to make the recipe unique.

Need a way to brighten up a cloudy day? Creamy Dreamy Cloud Salad does the trick. You'll think you're eating a cloud when you bite into this fluffy, colorful combination.

DIFFICULTY LEVEL: ★ ☆ ☆
SERVING SIZE: 6–8

CREAMY DREAMY CLOUD SALAD

WHAT YOU NEED

•• Ingredients

1 (15-ounce) can fruit cocktail
1 (3-ounce) box pistachio instant pudding mix
1 (8-ounce) container whipped topping
1 (16-ounce) bag mini marshmallows
1 cup slivered almonds

•• Tools

colander

large mixing bowl

rubber scraper

1 Open a can of fruit cocktail. Drain the fruit into a colander.

2 In a large mixing bowl, stir together dry pudding mix, whipped topping, and mini marshmallows with a rubber scraper.

3 Add fruit cocktail to the mixing bowl and stir ingredients together.

4 Chill the mixture in the refrigerator for one hour.

5 Just before serving, sprinkle the slivered almonds on top of the salad.

For a nice crunch in every bite, stir in the almonds just before serving. You can also replace the fruit cocktail with canned pineapple or pears.

While salads are usually side dishes, this one is perfect to serve as a main course. Your taste buds are in for a treat with the unique flavors of this Asian-inspired dish.

ASIAN CHICKEN SALAD

WHAT YOU NEED

●● Ingredients

6 chicken nuggets
5 green onions
1 bag shredded cabbage
2 tablespoons sesame seeds
½ cup sliced almonds
2 packages chicken flavored ramen noodles
½ cup vegetable oil
1 tablespoon sugar
3 tablespoons vinegar
½ teaspoon salt
½ teaspoon pepper

●● Tools

baking sheet

cutting board

paring knife

large mixing bowl

oven mitts

pot holder

small bowl

whisk

1 Place the chicken nuggets on a baking sheet and bake according to package instructions.

2 On a cutting board, cut off the white part and the top ¼ of the onions with a paring knife. Throw these away. Cut the rest of the green onions into ¼-inch slices. Put the slices in a large mixing bowl.

3 Use an oven mitt or pot holder to remove baking sheet from the oven. Allow nuggets to cool for 10–15 minutes.

4 On the cutting board, cut each nugget into four pieces and put them in the mixing bowl. Add cabbage, sesame seeds, and almonds to the bowl.

5 Remove the flavor packets from the ramen noodles. Break the noodles apart into the large mixing bowl.

6 In a small bowl, add oil, sugar, vinegar, salt, pepper, and the flavor packets from the ramen noodles. Combine ingredients with a whisk.

7 Pour mixture over the salad. Fold ingredients until the salad is completely covered with dressing.

Tasty Tips

You can give this salad a different taste by changing a few ingredients. If you don't like cabbage, use a bag of shredded lettuce instead. You can also try different flavored ramen noodles.

TOOLS GLOSSARY

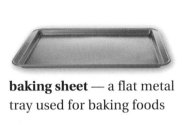

baking sheet — a flat metal tray used for baking foods

fork — an eating utensil often used to stir or mash

mixing spoon — a large spoon with a wide, circular end used to mix ingredients

colander — a bowl-shaped strainer used for washing or draining food

melon baller — a kitchen tool with a rounded end used for scooping out balls of melon

oven mitt — a large mitten made from heavy fabric used to protect hands when removing hot pans from the oven

cutting board — a wooden or plastic board used when slicing or chopping foods

mixing bowl — a sturdy bowl used for mixing ingredients

paring knife — a small, sharp knife used for peeling or slicing

pot holder — a thick, heavy fabric cut into a square or circle that is used to remove hot pans from the oven

rubber scraper — a kitchen tool with a rubber paddle on the end

saucepan — a deep pot with a handle

sharp knife — a kitchen knife with long blade used to cut ingredients

skillet — a flat pan used to cook non-liquid foods on a stovetop

small bowl — a bowl used for mixing a small amount of ingredients

spatula — a kitchen tool with a broad, flat metal or plastic blade at the end, used for removing food from a pan

vegetable peeler — a small tool with two blades used to remove peels from vegetables and fruits

whisk — a metal tool used for beating ingredients

GLOSSARY

brown (BROUN) — to cook something until its color becomes brown

combination (KAHM-buh-nay-shun) — a mixture of two or more things together

fiesta (fee-ESS-tuh) — a holiday or religious festival, especially in Spanish-speaking countries

fold (FOHLD) — to mix or add ingredients by gently turning the light ingredient over the heavy ingredient

unique (yoo-NEEK) — one of a kind

variation (vair-ee-AY-shuhn) — something that is slightly different from another thing of the same type

READ MORE

Betty Crocker Kids Cook! Hoboken, N.J.: Wiley, 2007.

Graimes, Nicola. *Kids' Fun and Healthy Cookbook.* New York: DK, 2007.

Ibbs, Katharine. *I Can Cook!* New York: DK, 2007.

INTERNET SITES

FactHound offers a safe, fun way to find Internet sites related to this book. All of the sites on FactHound have been researched by our staff.

Here's how:
1. Visit *www.facthound.com*
2. Choose your grade level.
3. Type in this book ID **1429613416** for age-appropriate sites. You may also browse subjects by clicking on letters, or by clicking on pictures and words.
4. Click on the **Fetch It** button.

FactHound will fetch the best sites for you!

ABOUT THE AUTHOR

Kristi Johnson got her start in the kitchen when she was a little girl helping her mom, aunt, and grandmas with cooking and baking. Over the years, she decided that her true passion was baking. She spent many days in the kitchen covering every countertop with her favorite chocolate chip cookies.

Kristi attended the baking program at the Le Cordon Bleu College of Culinary Arts in Minnesota. After graduating with highest honors, Kristi worked in many restaurants and currently works in the baking industry.

INDEX